THIS BOOK BELONGS TO:

_____

Thank you Amy Borie and Laurel Morais
for your expert evaluation and critique.

For Aubrey,
& for dream chasers everywhere - find
your true wind and stay the course.
- KT

To Zack, Zoe, & my mother, Renee,
whose presence in my life continues
to ignite my zeal for creativity.
- JW

First Whisper Sea Company Press Hardcover Edition 2019

WHISPER SEA COMPANY PRESS
An imprint of Whisper Sea Company, LLC
St. Augustine, FL 32080

For information about this title contact the publisher:
Whisper Sea Company Press
wscstudio@outlook.com

Library of Congress Control Number: 2019911420

ISBN:
Hardcover: 978-1-7333829-0-8
Paperback: 978-1-7333829-1-5

Stella's Tale

OF Sea & Sail

BY

KELLY TURNER

ILLUSTRATED BY

JACQUE WATSON

Under fickle skies, on a coquina shore,
in the town of St. Augustine,
lived a little girl, with *wavy hair*,
in a house painted Key-Lime Green.

Every day, whether sunny or gray,
on the front porch Stella would be,
watching the white sails and the
white caps play *peek-a-boo* on the sea.

Oh, how she wished that it were she,
upon a *heaving deck*;
sun on her face, wind in her hair,
and sea-spray on her neck.

One night she tucked in
with a sailing book,
her covers piled on in a heap.
Eagerly she read *page after page*,
while reading she soon fell asleep.

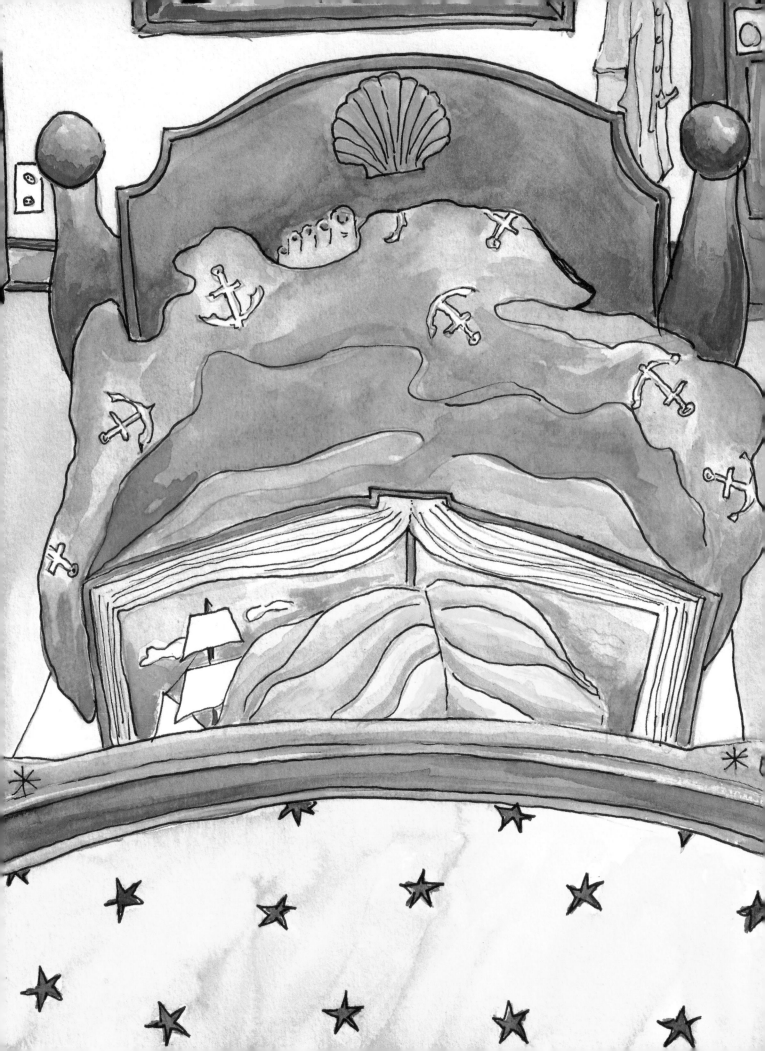

In the night she awoke to a CREAK
CLANK
CLUNK

and a *tingle* in the pit of her belly.
She fumbled her way out of bed in the dark,
beneath her, her legs felt like jelly.

Her heart skipped a beat
and jumped into her throat,
with each shudder and *lurch of the floor*.
She staggered toward a dark oval shape,
found a latch and opened a door.

Outside in the sun
was a wide teak deck,
with masts rising up to the sky.
Above was a maze of cables and spars,
with white sails that *seemed to fly*.

FRANK

"Good Morning young Mate,"
bellowed a sinewy man,
his voice - sharp as a razor.
With a broad smile and a wink, he said,

CARLOS

"Welcome aboard
          the Stargazer."

AMANDA

"I'm Karl, the ship's Bosun," he offered,
tapping his chest with a pat,
then pointed out the *Main Mast crew*,
"Frank, Carlos, Amanda, and Matt."

MATT

Frank took the lead to show Stella the ship,
she learned at a furious pace,
the names of the sails, the lines and the rig;
words like: *luff, leech, sheet, clew, and brace.*

Stella memorized sailing commands,
there were so many phrases to know.
Unfolding like a synchronized dance,

"LET FALL"

"READY ABOUT"

"WEAR 'O."

In a magnetic rhythm, the Stargazer's
crew set in motion a grand ballet;
some lines were *pulled*, some *made-fast*,
others they let *run away.*

The Stargazer pitched, rolled into a heel
in the fine suit of sails that she wore.
The crew let out a cheer,

HIP, HIP, HUZZAH!

then set about their daily chores.

Stella's work list was long and detailed:
climb aloft, swab the decks, splice line;
weave baggywrinkle, mend the t'gallant sail,
and give the *ship's brass* a shine.

Stella took the helm that afternoon,
watching the sails against the sky;
keeping them filled,
driving close to the wind,
sailing Stargazer *full and by.*

The skies grew suddenly dark and gray;
the crew began to *douse sail*.
The sea whipped into a frenzied froth;
the wind blew a ferocious gale.

Stella pushed the wheel, it pushed her back;
her muscles felt like rubber-bands.
With every ounce of srength she had,
she leaned in and hardened her stance.

As quick as it stirred, the ocean calmed,
and as far as Stella could see,
parting clouds displayed an evening sky,
only witnessed at sea.

The crescent moon was barely aglow;
sails shimmering in the night.
For the heavens were ablaze,
with infinite *twinkling lights*.

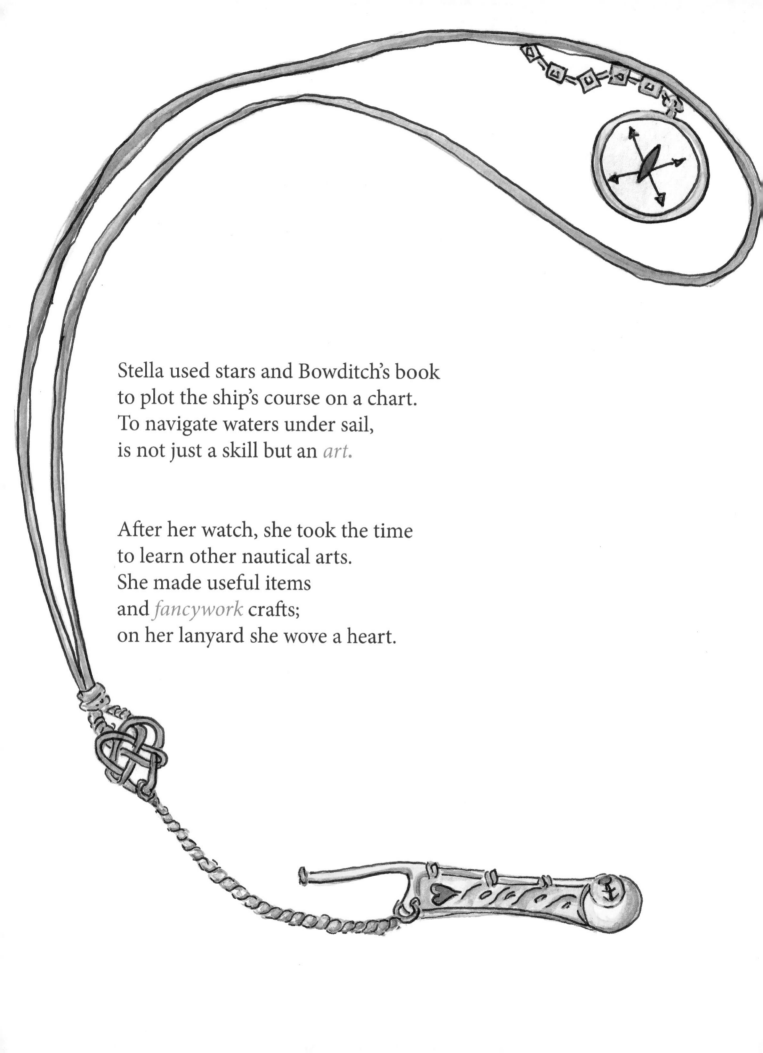

Stella used stars and Bowditch's book
to plot the ship's course on a chart.
To navigate waters under sail,
is not just a skill but an *art*.

After her watch, she took the time
to learn other nautical arts.
She made useful items
and *fancywork* crafts;
on her lanyard she wove a heart.

Stargazer anchored,
the very next morning,
in a tranquil turquoise bay.
Rising out of the water
in a *brilliance of color*,
the island of Bermuda lay.

Bleached white roofs
dotted lush green hills,
capping houses in every *hue*;
cobalt, yellow, coral, and pink,
chartreuse and periwinkle blue.

Stella packed up the sea-bag she'd made
out of sailcloth, twine, and leather.
She set out to explore the *pink-sand* beach,
and bask in the balmy weather.

Boat by lazy boat the crew came,
back at the end of the day;
bronze on their skin, pink-sand
on their feet, ready to get *underway*.

Stella snuggled into her canvas cocoon,
eyelids heavy with each gentle sway.
She smiled as the waves lulled her to sleep;
contented, she **drifted** away.

Stella woke in the morning,
as she had many times,
to the *tinking and clinking*
of her copper wind-chimes.

She sighed a *long sigh*,
she was home, it would seem.
It felt so real;
was it all just a dream?

As she pushed back her covers
her book *fell to the floor*;
on the page was a picture
of a ship's oval door.

Just then she noticed,
crumpled up like a rag,
on the floor by her bed,
lay a hand stitched *sea-bag*.

Bounding up from her bed,
over to it she ran;
it was empty inside...

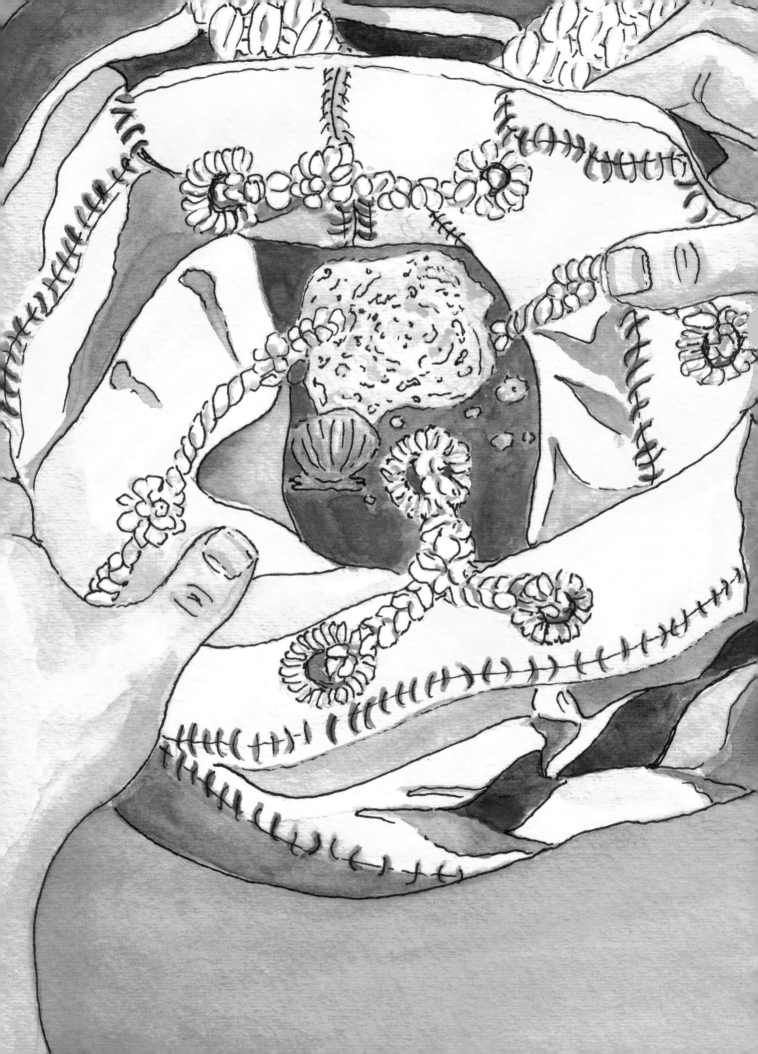

... but for a little *pink-sand.*

Glossary

Avast: command to immediately stop (typically used in emergencies

Baggywrinkle: fuzzy wraps around rigging, installed to prevent sails from chaffing on the rigging

Belay: to "make-fast" or tie-off a line securely

Bermuda: British Island territory located at 30.3078 N 64.7505 W

Block: Part of a pully system that a line or rope passes through to obtain mechanical advantage

Bos'n / Bosun (Boatswain): a ship's officer in charge of equipment and crew

Bowditch: Nathaniel Bowditch, an early American mathematician who revolutionized ocean navigation, and is considered the founder of modern maritime navigation; his book The New American Practical Navigator, first published in 1802, is still carried on board every commissioned U.S. Coast Guard and Navy vessel.

Brace: line on a square-rigged ship to rotate a yard around the mast so the ship may sail at different angles to the wind

Celestial Navigation: navigation by using the sun, moon, and stars

Chart: ocean map on which a ships position is recorded / plotted

Clew: the lower or aft (rear) corner of a sail where the sheet is attached

Coquina: a soft limestone of broken shells

Douse: to take in sail

Ear: upper corners of a square sail

Eye: loop placed into a line by splicing

Fancywork: ornamental braiding or weaving

Foot: lower edge of a sail

Full & By: sailing close to the wind with sails filling

Head: upper edge of a square sail, the top of a mast, or the bow of a ship

Hove-to (Heave-to): stopping a ship

Heel: to be tilted over due to pressure from the wind

Jib: triangular staysail set forward of the forwardmost mast

Jibe: to change a vessel's course when sailing with the wind by causing the stern to pass through the eye of the wind by swinging the boom to the opposite side

Leech: vertical edge of a square sail & leeward edge of a fore-aft sail

Let Fall: command to push sails into their gear for setting

Line: rope that is in service

Luff: the edge of a fore-aft sail next to the stay

Lanyard: a cord tied around an object (knife, whistle, marlinspike)

Navigate: plan and direct the route of a ship

Pitch: alternating up-down movement of a ship's bow and stern

Ready About: command to "tack" or turn the ship by passing the bow through the wind

Rig (Rigging): system of ropes, cables, & chains which support a ships masts, spars, and sails

Sea-bag: duffle type bag made by sailors to carry their gear

Sextant: an instrument used for measuring angular distances between objects

Sheet: line attached to the clew of a sail, used to set and trim

Splice: join or connect rope by the interweaving of strands

Saint Augustine: oldest city in the USA, discovered by Ponce de Leon while searching for the Fountain of Youth

That's Well: non-emergency command to stop

T'gallant (Top Gallant): setion of the mast on a square rigged ship immediately above the Top Mast; the first sail set on this section of mast is the t'gallant sail.

Swab: a mop (noun) to mop (verb); also slang for a new crewmember

Underway: when a vessel is moving through the water

Wear 'O: command to "wear" or turn the ship by passing the stern through the wind (requires more sea room than a tack)

Yard / Yardarm: a spar on a mast from which sails are set.

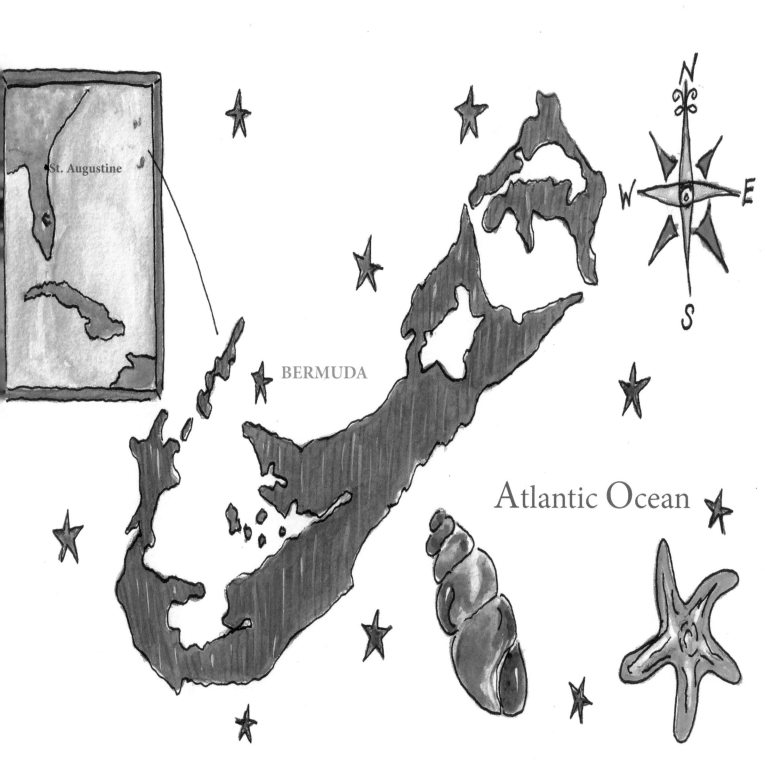

St. Augustine

BERMUDA

Atlantic Ocean

Kelly Turner (née Nixon)

Born in San Diego, but raised in the high desert of Joshua Tree, California - Kelly relished every moment she spent by the sea. As a child she imagined the vast expanse of desert was the undulating ocean.

At 20, Kelly joined the U.S. Coast Guard with the dream that she would one day crew the Tall Ship Eagle. Undaunted by rumors that Eagle, "doesn't take girls," Kelly requested and was selected as a part of Eagle's 1998 temporary summer crew. When an unexpected vacancy arose that Autumn, Kelly was asked back to Eagle as permanent crew - becoming Eagle's **_first female_** Permanent Crew Boatswain's Mate & Mast Captain.

"Always do your best work - a temporary dream assignment turned into the realization of my goals through hard, consistent work and dedication. Someone is _always_ paying attention. I took it seriously and was rewarded accordingly. Never let anyone tell you that you can't; I am living proof that you _can_."

Kelly lives in St. Augustine Beach, Florida with her husband Colin, and their two children, Jamison and Aubrey - and of course her old friend, the Sea.

Jacque Watson

Jacque's journey began on the water. Cayman born, she was surrounded by water living on her parent's 42' sailboat. Her artistic acumen developed early in her life, guided by her mother Renee's love of creativity and fervor for imagination.

Jacque began formal fine art training in high school and continued at Flagler College in St. Augustine, Florida. Her influences are largely derived from the places where she has lived and traveled. From her time spent on the islands, to her life in Florida, and through her journeys all over the world, Jacque has developed an eclectic toolkit from which she draws inspiration.

Her zeal for life and art have led her to embark on a variety of artistic endeavors. For Jacque, doing a children's book came naturally, as it is a medium through which she communicates her youthful spirit.

"I've always enjoyed a sense of whimsy in my art and I like to keep things light."

Presently, Jacque resides on Anastasia Island in St. Augustine, Florida with her two children, Zack and Zoe.

3/P